MOUSE GUARD
FALL 1152

MOUSE GUARD
FALL 1152

STORY & ART BY

DAVID PETERSEN

VILLARD • NEW YORK

2008 Villard Books Trade Paperback Edition

Published in the United States by Villard Books, an imprint of The Random House Publishing Group, a division of Random House, Inc., New York.

VILLARD and "V" CIRCLED Design are registered trademarks of Random House, Inc.

Originally published in hardcover and in slightly different form in the United States by Archaia Studios Press in 2007.

The chapters in this book first appeared in the comic book *Mouse Guard,* © and TM 2005 by David Peterson and published by Archaia Studios Press.

ISBN: 978-0-345-49686-7

www.villard.com

Printed in China on acid free paper

10 9 8 7

PREFACE

IN THE FOLLOWING PAGES YOU WILL FIND THE FIRST IN A SERIES OF ADVENTURE STORIES I CONCEIVED OVER TEN YEARS AGO. ON A SCRAP OF PAPER I HAD QUICKLY SCRATCHED "MICE HAVE A CULTURE ALL THEIR OWN; TOO SMALL TO INTEGRATE WITH OTHER ANIMALS." THIS SCRIBBLE LED TO MORE THOUGHT ABOUT HOW MICE WOULD SURVIVE AS CHARACTERS IN SUCH A HOSTILE WORLD POPULATED WITH PREDATORS: "HIDE THE CITIES, MAKE THEM SELF-SUFFICIENT AND SPREAD APART FROM ONE ANOTHER." FROM A STORYTELLING PERSPECTIVE, IT MEANT THE MICE WERE PRISONERS OF THEIR OWN HOMES.

SKETCHES FOLLOWED OF THREE MICE, SAXON, KENZIE, AND RAND, DESTINED TO PLAY THE ROLES OF PATHFINDERS FOR THEIR KIND. AS MOUSE GUARD RATTLED AROUND IN MY HEAD, THE WORLD BECAME POPULATED WITH MORE CHARACTERS, TOWNS AND VILLAGES, AND A HISTORY OF ITS OWN, UNTIL 2005 WHEN IT BEGAN SPILLING ONTO PAPER.

I AM VERY HAPPY TO BEGIN SHARING THAT WORLD.

I WISH TO EXPRESS SPECIAL THANKS TO MY PARENTS, JESSE GLENN, MIKE DAVIS, EMERSON JONES, SEYTH MIERSMA, JEREMY BASTIAN, MAIJA GRAHAM, NATE PRIDE, RICK CORTES, MARK SMYLIE, AKI LIAO, BRIAN PETKASH & GUY DAVIS.

David Petersen

DAVID PETERSEN
MICHIGAN 2007

FOR MY WIFE, JULIA

AND IN LOVING MEMORY OF
GILBERT AND DORIS PETERSON

Contents

CHAPTER ONE

BELLY OF THE BEAST

The mice struggle to live safely and prosper among all of the world's harsh conditions and predators. Thus the Mouse Guard was formed. After persevering against a weasel warlord in the winter war of 1149, the territories are no longer as troubled. True, the day-to-day dangers exist, but no longer are the Guard soldiers, instead they are escorts, pathfinders, weather watchers, scouts and body guards for the mice who live among the territories. Many skills are necessary for the guard to keep the borders safe. They must find new safeways and paths from village to village, lead shipments of goods from one town to another and, in case of attack, guard against all evil and harm to their territories.

'Hail all those who are able,
any mouse can,
any mouse will,
but the Guard prevail'

LET ME TELL YE ABOUT THE GUARD. WE MICE HAVE LITTLE CHANCE IN THIS WORLD, CONSIDERING ALL THE CRITTERS THAT EATS US.

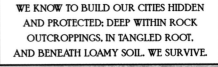

WE KNOW TO BUILD OUR CITIES HIDDEN AND PROTECTED; DEEP WITHIN ROCK OUTCROPPINGS, IN TANGLED ROOT, AND BENEATH LOAMY SOIL. WE SURVIVE.

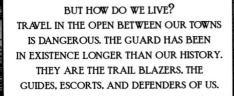

BUT HOW DO WE LIVE? TRAVEL IN THE OPEN BETWEEN OUR TOWNS IS DANGEROUS. THE GUARD HAS BEEN IN EXISTENCE LONGER THAN OUR HISTORY. THEY ARE THE TRAIL BLAZERS, THE GUIDES, ESCORTS, AND DEFENDERS OF US.

I SELL GRAIN FROM ROOTWALLOW TO BARKSTONE,
I KNOW THE WAY AND FOLLOW THE PATHS I'VE BEEN SHOWN.
THE GUARD IS TOO NECESSARY IN OTHER PLACES
TO TOUR THIS OLDFUR AROUND.

JUST NEED TO STOP FOR A BIT...

MOUSE GUARD:
Belly of the Beast

GWENDOLYN SAID YOU WOULD BRIEF US ONCE WE WERE ON THE TRAIL, KENZIE. SO TELL US, WHY HAVE THREE OF THE GUARD'S FINEST BEEN DISPATCHED?

LIEAM

A MOUSE PEDDLING GRAIN TOOK THE PATH FROM ROOTWALLOW TO BARKSTONE ALONE.

WE NEED TO FIND THIS MISSING GRAIN MOUSE...

SEEMS HE NEVER ARRIVED AT HIS DESTINATION.

KENZIE

WE WON'T AT THIS RATE... IT'S STILL QUITE A WAY TO BARKSTONE AND NO SIGN OF THE LOST FOOL YET.

SAXON

WE SHOULD BE PRESSING ON.

I AGREE, BUT PERHAPS A VIEW WILL TELL US *WHERE* TO PRESS, EH?

SEE ANYTHING UP THERE, REDFUR?

I SEE A CART!

Chapter Two

Shadows Withn

While Saxon, Kenzie, and Lieam were tracking the path of the grain merchant, Gwendolyn, head of the Mouse Guard, sent word to Sadie. Sadie, who once watched a shoreline region of the Mouse Territories, has been asked to make contact with another missing mouse, Guard member Conrad. There has been no outgoing communication from his shoreline dwelling, Calogero, and the Guard fear the worst...

'Send any mouse to do the job, it may or may not be done. Ask the Guard to do the task, even death cannot prevent it from completion.'

THE NORTHERN SHORE.

YOU WERE OUT FOR A FEW HOURS.

. . . . .

SOME SOUP WILL BE GOOD FOR YOU.

THEN YOU CAN TELL ME ABOUT THIS "TRAITOR."

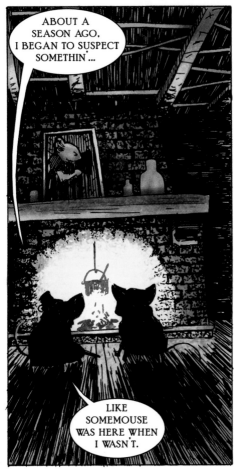

ABOUT A SEASON AGO, I BEGAN TO SUSPECT SOMETHIN'...

LIKE SOMEMOUSE WAS HERE WHEN I WASN'T.

?!

CONRAD, IT'S MID-MORNING AND CALOGERO IS STILL DARK...

SOMETHING IS BLOCKING THE WINDOWS!

AND THE DOOR!

THERE IS ANOTHER WAY OUT!

TRICKED YA!

CHAPTER THREE

RISE OF THE AXE

Saxon, Kenzie, and Lieam, having abandoned the grain cart, have opted to take a lesser known path to the city of Barkstone, hoping to keep as low a profile as possible. What worries them more than knowing of a traitor is not knowing who the traitor is. They are unaware of the information Sadie carries with her to Lockhaven, or the fate of fellow Guard, Conrad.

"Take not the duty of the Guard lightly.
Friends must not be enemies
Just as enemies must not be friends.
Discerning the two is a life's work."

--From the writings of Laria
4th Lockhaven Guard Matron

ANY LUCK?

NO LEADS.

ARE WE BEING FOLLOWED?

GOOD ENOUGH DISTRACTION?

I CAN ONLY HOPE.

DID YOU SEE THAT?!

OH!

GET UP!

HIS STAFF COULD SPLIT.

?

THAT LITTLE ONE HAS FIRE IN HIM.

THE TALL GREYFUR CAN HOLD HIS OWN.

KNOCK HIM DOWN!

CHAPTER FOUR

THE DARK GHOST

Hiding within the ranks of the mysterious militia
known only as 'the Axe', Lieam is unaware
that his Guard companions, Kenzie and
Saxon, have been left for dead outside
Barkstone's gates. Celanawe, a hermit
and stranger to the mouse cities,
has retrieved the red and blue
cloaked mice and dragged them to
his secluded home...and a
dark plot quietly grows.

*'Death is as powerful a weapon
as it is an easy escape.
Heroes can pass in to legend,
Legends into myths,
Myths fuel new heroes.'*

-the last recorded words of the Black Axe:
Champion of the Mouse Guard

CHAPTER FIVE

MIDNIGHT'S DAWN

In tracking the treacherous Axe army, Saxon and Kenzie found a new ally in an old hermit mouse named Celanawe claiming to be the ancient hero of the mice: The Black Axe. His fate intertwined with two of the Guard's finest, he offered to aid them in their pursuit in hopes to hold them to their word of retrieving his missing axe.

All the while, Lieam's captors march him to Lockhaven with only one purpose: to conquer it.

'Clouds, leaves, soil, and wind
all offer themselves as signals
of changes in the weather.
However, not all the storms of life
can be predicted.

-Excerpt from 'Weather Watcher's Field Guide'
distributed to all Guard Mice

THE GUARD HAS BEEN BETRAYED.

MIDNIGHT, THE GUARD'S WEAPONSMITH, REVEALED HIMSELF AS THE COMMANDER OF THIS ARMY:

"THE AXE."

HE TAUNTED ME WITH THREATS OF DEATH...

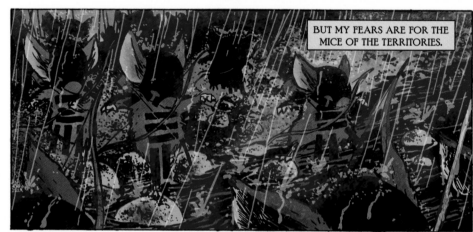

BUT MY FEARS ARE FOR THE MICE OF THE TERRITORIES.

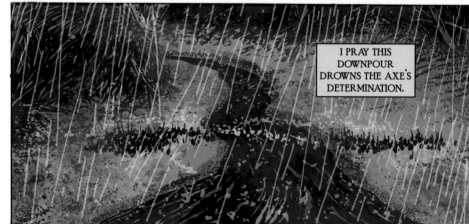

I PRAY THIS DOWNPOUR DROWNS THE AXE'S DETERMINATION.

Before the days of peace the guard needed every mouse brave enough to stand and rise above the villains of the territories. One mouse alone bore the brunt of the task. An axe of black severed the necks of the five serpents who surrounded all that is. Thus begins his tale.

The axe itself was forged into being by the blacksmith Farrer. His family had been slain by predators whilst weaponless.

Hotter coals have never since been bellowed, and every strike of his hammer into the ore was a strike unto his enemies. Thus the black axe was forged.

The weapon proved too heavy to wield. It held the burden of all the blacksmith's mourning. To find a true hero it was taken to **Lockhaven**.

O ne mouse of lockhaven took the great axe and vowed to defend the weak and hunt his predators

his true name kept secret, he took the title of his weapon the Black Axe

MERITT, WHY IS THE PORTCULLIS STILL RAISED!?

IT'S A PULLEY, SIR. MUST BE THIS RAIN RUSTING THE WORKS.

BRACE THE DOORS WITH ANYTHING AND EVERYTHING!

SADIE, YOU CAN TELL GWENDOLYN MORE OF WHAT YOU KNOW IN HER STUDY.

CHAPTER SIX

A RETURN TO HONOR

Lockhaven is under siege. The home of the Mouse Guard has been assaulted by many a predator, but rarely has it stood in opposition to mice. Rand, the defense expert of the Guard's home, received just enough warning from Sadie to seal the gates and secure the fortress before it came under treasonous attack.

Saxon & Kenzie, along with the oldfur Celanawe, also unable to get into Lockhaven, are forced to hide in the low maples to the east and watch their beloved home betrayed.

'Let this stone always stand for
safety and prosperity.
Let it be your conviction,
your pride, and your home.'
*-Dedication recited by all Mouse Guard Matriarchs
to new Guard mice upon entering Lockhaven*

A 'REDFUR' SETTLING A SCORE.

EPILOGUE

Midnight's concerns over the order of authority between the Guard, the towns and the villages, were valid.

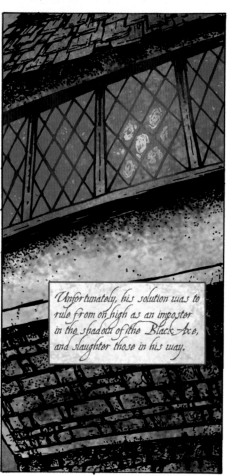

Unfortunately, his solution was to rule from on high as an imposter in the shadow of the Black Axe, and slaughter those in his way.

Mouse should never raise blade against mouse. There are enough outside threats in this world.

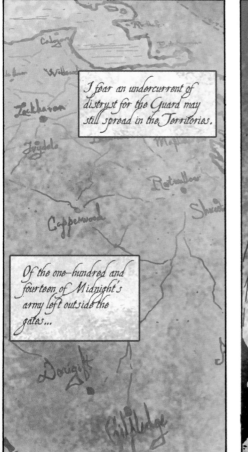

I fear an undercurrent of distrust for the Guard may still spread in the Territories.

Of the one-hundred and fourteen of Midnight's army left outside the gates...

most went back to their homes and lives,

as though nothing had happened.

Only three were imprisoned by their local magistrates. The rest walk freely.

As for the Guard involved in this ordeal...

Rand's leg never fully healed from the winter war two years ago.

The wound worsened in the battle with Midnight's army and he almost lost his leg.

After serving many seasons out on patrol and in charge of Lockhaven's defenses, he is now bound to a crutch.

Our healers have confirmed he will never be able to patrol again and will remain in Lockhaven for the rest of his time with the Guard.

Sadie was lonely for far too long when she was stationed at the shore outpost of Frostic.

It is good to have her return to Lockhaven as a patrol mouse again.

It's too remote and far a journey to risk sending a Guard through this weather, when there is much to be done in populated areas.

Conrad's death has isolated her, though.

She was determined to recover his remains and secure Calogero, but I have to forbid it at this time.

I have advised her to seek the camaraderie of her fellow Guard mice.

Saxon and Kenzie are both the best of friends and most bitter of rivals.

I group Guard mice whose skills compliment each other.

I rarely send either of them away without the other.

They are two of my finest Guard mice.

Their duties keep them away from Lockhaven.

It's rare that so many of the patrol mice would all be here at the same time.

Beds are cold more often than they are used.

Lieam, only recruited in 1149, is the most promising I have seen in my time at Lockhaven.

I fear the horrors of what he has been through are forcing him to grow up quicker than most.

Though, he does seem to be taking it all in stride.

The sudden return of an old hero has given him a new mentor.

Celanawe. Records indicate that he was at one time a Guard...

But, mention of him suddenly ceases.

He claims to be the true Black Axe but has told me in confidence it is to remain a secret between those who witnessed Midnight's attempt on my life.

The Guard and I are in great debt to him. I have offered him the sanctuary of Lockhaven as a home for the time being.

It's thrilling to think the Black Axe is more than a legend...

A myth made real.

Tonight, I will leave them all to their enjoyment of Lockhaven's warmth as a home, but in the coming days, I will send them out again.

ONLY WHAT YE NEED AND NOT A MORSEL MORE

Our weather watchers tell us this first snow will blanket the territories by morning...

and Lockhaven is woefully short on supplies needed for a long harsh winter.

-Guendolyn
first snowfall 1152

Maps, Guides, and Assorted Extras

Mouse Territories 1150

A map of cities, towns, villages, and safepaths after the winter war

As measured by the Guard of 1149, Recorded by Clarke's Cartography

Fallen settlements listed & struck

Calogero

Dawnrock

Darkheather
Entrance

Whitepine

Thistledown

Wildseed

Elmwood

Lockhaven

Ironwood

Pebblebrook

Shaleburrow

Blackrock

Barkstone

Ivydale

Woodruff's Grove

Elmoss

Roo

Copperwood

Ferndale

Scout Border

Sprucetuck

Darkheather
Tunnels

Walnutpeck

Dorigift

Appleloft

Gilpledge

BARKSTONE:

This town is located on the Western end of the Mouse Territories. Its gates were built into the trunk of a Locust tree backed up to an outcropping of stone. The town lies inside.

Known for being home to artisans and craftsmice, Barkstone is the destination for the best in glass, furniture, and other goods.

LOCKHAVEN:

Home of the Mouse Guard. Carved deep into stone, only the face of Lockhaven is visible from the outside. It is also protected by a thick layer of ivy. Lockhaven serves as a base of operations for the Guard and is not a true city. While there are mouse citizens that live there, they are only there as invited guests of the Guard to perform certain skills and labors:

WEAPONS & ARMOR:

A full time smith is kept on hand at Lockhaven to mend, sharpen, and create weapons and tools for the Guard. Occasionally this job is held by a Guard, but often it proves too time consuming for a patrol mouse.

COOKERY:

Staple foods are stored in abundance, while prepared foods are made as needed, as it is unknown how many or few will be fed on any given day. Lockhaven is known for Gabcroon: a dense bread filled with seeds, fruits, and nuts. It travels well and stays warm long after baking.

TEXTILES:

Woven and sewn fabrics are important to the mice of Lockhaven. The Guard are known for their cloaks, which need to be both warm and durable, as they are a Guard's primary piece of clothing.

APIARY:

Lockhaven is also home to a hive of bees. The mice harvest the honey for food and the wax for goods and medicinal purposes. To do this, the Apiary Keeper uses smoke to charm the bees. The bees also serve as a natural deterrent to other predators.

COMMON MOUSE TRADES:

Stone Mason:
Once chiseled into shape, stone provides a useful building material for mouse settlements. Masons quarry, shape, and lay mortar for the stone.

Carpenter:
From the smallest project to the largest, wood is a vital resource available to mice. An adze is used to square a timber for construction.

Potter:
Clay collected from under the soil is shaped and fired to create many food preparation and storage vessels. Kilns are closely tended in order to keep the temperature inside high enough to fire the clay.

Miller:

Using the collected grain, a miller will use a stone gristmill to grind the harvest into a finer texture.

Baker:

Prepared foods can last longer and be stored and eaten more easily than raw grains. It also allows for the addition of seeds, nuts, and fruits to be added into a single-item meal.

Examples of Pottery:

a: plate with painted trim.
b: storage jar with dragonfly motif
c: water jug with stopper
d: teapot with wooden grip
e: small decorative water pitcher
f: personal bowl
g: personal bowl
h: serving dish with leaf motif
i: scented smoking vessel
j: heavy drinking mug

A GALLERY OF PINUPS

BY ESTEEMED AUTHORS & FRIENDS

AS PRESENTED IN THE
ORIGINAL MOUSE GUARD SERIES

Pinup by Guy Davis

Pinup by Guy Davis

Pinup by Rick Cortes & anjindesign.com

Pinup by Mark Smylie

Pinup by Jeremy Bastian

Pinup by Jeremy Bastian

ILLUSTRATION GALLERY